Dear Jackson

Carynn Bohley

TO PEOPLE WHO ARE LOOKING
FOR A LIGHT
IN THE DARKNESS.

Carynn Bohley

Chapter One

People say that life is full of opportunities. That it's a *gift*.

A temporary gift that we inherit from past generations and use only until it's time to hand it off to the younger idiots, who will most likely screw up without our sage guidance.

I've never heard anyone say the last part, but it's clearly true.

Here are three things that I've learned about life during my sixteen years of existence:

1. You can't keep completely unfair things from happening.

2. Only ten percent of the people you meet will actually like you for who you are, and that's only if they try to get to know you (which they usually don't).

3. To be blunt and sum up this short list, life sucks.

This is what I'm thinking about instead of listening to Judge Leroy Johnson, who rambles on about custody and legal agreements with my parents. I don't even pretend to be paying attention at this point, because let's face it: Two hours in a courtroom with your bratty little sister isn't the most entertaining thing in the world, especially when you didn't get a chance to use the bathroom before you rushed out the door because your mom wrote the time down wrong.

Annie tugs on my tie and tries to whisper something to me, but I push her hand away. She growls in that insolent, I-get-whatever-I-want-because-I'm-an-eight-year-old-diva way, and I roll my eyes. "What the heck do you want?"

Annie pushes her pale blonde hair behind her ears and says, "I don't understand what's going on."

I let out a dry laugh. "I guess there's a first time for everything." Annie glares at me, so I shrug. "It's boring legal stuff. They're just discussing right now."

"Discussing what?" Annie's usually bright brown eyes are hard and calculating.

"You know what," I mumble. "We've been over this."

Annie turns so she's fully facing me, the glare still intact. "No, no one's told me anything. You and Mom and Dad are just acting weird. It's like you don't want me to get upset, so you pretend everything is okay, even though it isn't. It's obvious."

"You're lucky Mom and Dad protect you the way they do. As for me, I don't tell you things because you don't need to know," I say flatly. "You talk too much as it is."

Annie huffs. "You're the biggest jerk ever. You're even worse than Toby Jacobs," she adds. "He calls people names and sticks his tongue out at the teacher when she isn't looking, and sometimes he even picks his nose." She shivers in disgust.

"Every eight year old picks their nose," I mutter tiredly.

"I don't."

"Whatever you say."

"I don't! I swear, I don't," Annie says defensively.

"You know what, Annie? I really don't care." I turn my back to her and stare at the fire exit on the opposite side of the room. It'd be so easy to jump out of this uncomfortable fold-up chair and take off. Of course, then there would be the question of *where would I go?*

I must start to doze off because after what seems to be a few moments Mom's shaking my shoulder, and the hearing is over. She doesn't say anything until we're in the car- just her, Annie and I- and I don't push her to. She doesn't start driving, doesn't even put the key in the ignition. A few lifetimes go by before she speaks, and her voice is quiet.

"I have full custody," she tells me.

This was to be expected. It's not like the judge would give our dad custody. At least, not until he gets his act together.

Dad is an alcoholic, and he hasn't kept a job for more than a few months at a time since I was Annie's age. It's no wonder that Mom finally decided to get divorced, but it still hurts. It's not like I'd admit it out loud, but it feels like I'm carrying bricks in my stomach.

"So Dad's moving out?"

Mom doesn't say anything for a few moments. Then, "No, Malcolm. *We're* moving out."

I feel like my wind's been knocked out. I can't force my mouth shut. I sit there gaping at her like an idiot for the next thirty seconds.

Only Annie finds her voice. "Where are we going to go?"

"That isn't fair," I begin, but then I remember my first rule of life. "I mean, you got custody, you should get the house too, right?"

"I chose to let your father keep the house."

I'm dumbfounded. Utterly dumbfounded. "What... why?" I manage to sputter.

Mom takes a deep breath. "Why don't we talk about this at home?"

"Why don't we talk about this now?" I demand.

Mom is rubbing her temples with her fingertips the way she always does when she's under a lot of stress. "Malcolm, this is hard on all of us. You need to think of people other than yourself."

Annie would usually stick her tongue out at me, but when I glance in her direction she's sitting quietly with her hands folded in her lap, her eyes trained out the window. I turn back to Mom, and her tired eyes meet mine in the visor.

"I'm sorry," I mumble. "I just want to know what's going on."

"And you will," Mom assures me. "Just as soon as we get home. I think what we all need is a cold glass of lemonade."

I sit back in my seat. "That sounds good," I say with forced calm.

I'm the man of the family now. I know that making things hard on Mom is completely unfair to her. Unlike my life, that's something I can control.

. . .

Annie and Mom sit on the couch in the living room- our living room, the one we shouldn't be moving out of just because my dad is a mega jerk- and I sit in an armchair across from them.

"So what's the deal?" I blurt out, because God didn't bless me with the gift of patience.

"Your grandmother's been going through a hard time since Grandpa passed away last year. She's lonely," Mom begins, and right away I know where this is going. I try to interrupt her, but my voice seems to be stuck in my throat. "That job offer I got last month... the pay is

good, and it's in the town right next to your
grandmother's-"

Now I do speak up. "Mom, you want to move to
Kentucky? Don't you think it's a little... I don't know,
extreme? And do I look like I should be living in the
country?" I don't know what about me looks non-
country-ish, but I say it anyway. "None of us are meant
for that kind of life. It just isn't for us."

Mom smiles. "You're forgetting that I grew up in
Kentucky."

"I'm not forgetting. You live here in
Massachusetts now, don't you? You could've stayed in
the country if you wanted to, but you didn't."

Mom's eyes are distant. "I left to be with your
father." She frowns. "I shouldn't have left... I see that
now. And here's the perfect opportunity to go back."

"But what about school?" I mumble hopelessly,
even though we both know that, one, I don't care one bit
about school, and two, the school year will be over in
less than two weeks anyway.

"You'll go to the school near Grandma's house
in the fall, as will Annie," Mom replies.

I hack my brain for any other excuse. "Have you
even talked to Grandma about this? She might be a bit
surprised if we just show up on her doorstep and expect
her to take us in."

Mom sets down her cup of lemonade. "Of
course I have. I talked to her about it after I got the job

offer. I've been considering moving for a while now, but I didn't want to talk to you about it until I was sure I'd get custody."

Anger rises in my throat. "This whole time you've been considering this, and now you tell us? When do you plan to move, next week?"

Mom bites her lip. "Actually, the moving truck should be coming to pick up our stuff tomorrow."

"Oh, I see. You didn't actually care if we agreed. You already called the moving company because you just assumed we would!"

"Malcolm," Mom warns.

I storm to my room, knowing it's immature but not caring. This is too much to be thrown at us all at once. The worst part is, Annie seems fine with it.

I grab my laptop off of my desk and shoot an email to the one person who always takes my side.

Malcolm Gibbs <mal.a.Gibbs@gmail.com>
To Jackson-

Call me.

I pull out my phone and set it on my bed where I can access it easily, before digging through my closet for my mini basketball. When I find it, I sit down at the edge of my bed and start shooting it at the hoop on my door.

I try not to get my hopes up. As a deployed soldier, Jackson rarely gets my emails in time to respond while I'm still online, let alone have a phone conversation.

Still, I can't help but check back to the phone every few minutes for missed calls. When it begins to ring, I nearly throw it across the room in surprise.

"Thank God, Jackson," I groan the moment I answer it.

"What is it this time?" Jackson asks, and I can hear the smile in his voice. "Did Annie eat the rest of the mint ice cream again?"

"Funny," I reply dryly. I sit back down at the edge of my bed and sigh. "Today was the trial."

"Oh."

"Yeah. Mom got custody, obviously."

"Where's Dad now?" Jackson asks.

I attempt to spin the mini basketball on my finger and fail. "He's staying at a hotel right now."

"So… where's he gonna go?"

My stomach clenches in anger. "That's why I wanted to talk to you. He's not going *anywhere*. Mom, Annie and I are moving in with Grandma."

"Woah. That's… big," Jackson says in surprise. "When is this happening?"

"Tomorrow, apparently," I mutter. "I tried to talk Mom out of it, but she won't change her mind. It's like she's homesick all of the sudden."

Jackson's end of the line is silent.

"You there?" I ask after a moment.

"Yeah, just thinking," Jackson says quickly.

"And?"

"Well, I don't know," Jackson admits. "It does seem a little out of nowhere."

I toss the basketball again. "That's what I said. It turns out that Mom's been thinking about it for a while and didn't bother to tell us until now."

"Hm. Well, maybe it'll be good for you."

I freeze. "What is that supposed to mean?"

"Don't get defensive. I was just trying to say that it's a good opportunity to… I don't know. Make friends? Figure out what you want to do with your life?"

"I don't know what moving to Kentucky has to do with either of those things," I mumble.

"Just give it a chance, bud. Try to have a positive mindset. And if you don't do it for yourself, do it for Mom. She's going through a hard time right now." I open my mouth to argue, but Jackson continues before I can. "Before you say something sarcastic, why don't you think about this from her point of view?"

I lay back on my pillow and sigh. "I'll try."

I hear Jackson's muffled voice as he draws back the phone to speak with someone. When he returns, he says, "Sorry Mal, I need to go. We'll talk later, okay?"

"Sure. Go do military stuff."

Jackson laughs. "Tell Annie I said I miss her. Bye."

I hang up the phone and toss it onto the end of my bed, before laying down and rubbing my eyes tiredly. I consider going to sleep now and skipping dinner, but finally force myself to get up and leave the room.

Mom and Annie are still on the couch, but now they study a photo album that Mom showed me a few years ago.

"I'm sorry," I say before I can change my mind.

Mom looks up and gives me a sad smile. "Thank you, Malcolm. I know this is hard, but I really think that this is the right decision."

"I know," I say, trying to see from her perspective like Jackson told me to. I inhale deeply, then release the breath. With as much enthusiasm as I can muster, I add, "I guess I should get packing."

"Wait, Mal, guess what?" Annie asks.

I hold in a sigh. I can only act patient for so long…

She holds out the photo album, and points to a picture of Mom standing beside her old pony, Liberty. "Mom said I can get a pony, just like she did when she was my age!"

I grit my teeth together, holding back the words I want to say because I know I shouldn't.

Don't you know why Mom agreed to that? I want to ask. *You and I are going to get everything we want so Mom can make up for divorcing Dad. Want a pony, Annie? Here you go! Two birthday gifts, two Christmas gifts... I know how it goes.*

Instead I say, "That's great, Annie," before turning on my heel and heading to my room to pack.

. . .

We pack for the rest of the afternoon. I stuff all of my belongings into bags and boxes and anything else I can find to carry it all in, though there isn't much. Other than my laptop, basketball and Michael Jordan posters, I wouldn't mind leaving it all here. Of course, I'll need my clothes and shoes as well.

Annie, on the other hand, seems to have packed up her whole room. Her clothes, her stuffed animals, her blankets and pillows, toys, costumes, her rock collection- yep, her whole room. I wouldn't be surprised if she smuggled her furniture into those bags, too.

"The moving truck will be here to get our stuff tomorrow," Mom reminds us, her face hidden by the giant box she's carrying. "For now we'll put everything in the entryway."

I feel a pang of sorrow at the thought of the entryway that's greeted me every time I've walked into this house for the past five years. I guess it's an exitway, now.

Sleep is impossible tonight. Whenever I start to drift off I'm startled awake by my thoughts. I'm afraid of what the future holds, and I'm also tormented by the present. I want to go back instead of going forward, back to the easy days of childhood.

The worst thing I ever had to worry about was having an empty water gun when I was playing with my friends, but that problem had an easy solution. Now I'm fighting on the battlefield they call life, and I'm holding an unfamiliar gun in my hands.

I'm unprepared for this; no one taught me how to shoot. I know how to aim at my targets, but sometimes it's hard to tell who the friend is and who the enemy is.

When I finally do fall asleep, I dream about war.

I'm fighting beside Jackson in Afghanistan. His uniform is torn and dirty, and his eyes have dark circles under them. He orders me to duck behind a rock, and I do as he says. I expect him to follow, but he stands with his feet planted on the earth and raises his gun toward our enemies.

I suck in a deep breath as a gunshot rings out, my hands flying to my ears at the deafening sound. When I look back to Jackson, I realize that he's fallen to the ground. Dark crimson waves run from a wound at his side, and he clutches it tightly.

He lets out an agonized groan, and suddenly I don't care about hiding. All that matters is keeping Jackson alive, and if I can't do that at least I can be with him when he dies. No one should ever die alone. Not good people, not bad people, and especially not Jackson.

My brother grips my hand tightly, his gray eyes full of pain that I wish I could take from him. It hurts more to see someone you love suffering than it does for you to endure the agony yourself.

"Listen, Malcolm," he says slowly, his words catching in shallow gasps.

"I'm listening," I assure him, my eyes stinging. I barely notice the bullets that tear through the air around us.

"You need to be there for Mom and Annie," Jackson continues, his eyes not leaving mine. "I love them so much, and so do you, even if you forget it sometimes. I know you're upset, but you have to remember... you're all they have. And you can keep them safe."

"I don't know if I can," I mumble, and I can't stop the tears from coming, now. I feel a sharp wave of pain fall over me as I crash forward, a bullet having burrowed itself into my side.

"Life will keep coming at you, Mal. It'll seem hopeless. Whatever happens, you need to stick through it. You need to fight back."

Another bullet, searing pain in my arm.

"Fight back," Jackson repeats.

Another.

"Fight back!"

And then I'm awake, sitting straight up in my bed and gasping as if there's no oxygen left in the room. Mom's standing in the doorway, her eyebrows drawn together in concern.

"Are you okay, honey?"

I try to make my breaths even and force a smile. "Yeah, I'm fine. Just a weird dream. What time is it?"

"Almost eight," she says with a smile. "The moving truck should be here soon!"

Chapter Two

Five minutes into the drive I want to hurl the GPS out the window.

'Turn... Left,' 'Turn... Right,' 'Turn Left... Then... Turn right. Turn right in five hundred feet. Turn right.' How am I going to survive a full day of riding in this little car with my suddenly talkative mother, Brat Kid and this freakishly annoying GPS?

"Who wants to play a game?" Mom asks enthusiastically. She hasn't stopped smiling since we left, and she hasn't snapped at either of us once. I wonder how long the good mood will last.

Annie kicks my seat in her excitement. "Me! What kind of game?"

"Stop kicking the back of my seat," I say dryly.

"Stop being so mean."

"Both of you stop," Mom orders, but she still wears a smile. "Annie, don't kick Malcolm's seat. Mal, be nice to your sister."

Now I imagine that Annie *is* sticking her tongue out at me, so I don't look at her, not wanting to give her

17

that satisfaction. Instead I stare out the passenger window, leaning my head against my arm and watching the world fly past. In a matter of hours, the urban will melt into suburban and the suburban will become rural. A matter of *many* hours, I remind myself, and decide to take a little nap so time will go by faster.

I get about forty-five minutes of sleep before Mom stops at the gas station.

"I have to go to the bathroom," Annie announces, so I reluctantly bring her inside while Mom fills the tank.

"I'll wait out here," I mutter, leaning back against a shelf of candy. I scoop up a pack of gum that's been knocked onto the floor and slip it into the pocket of my hoodie as casually as possible. I've never stolen anything before, and I expect to feel a sense of excitement from it. I need something, anything that will make me feel like I'm in control.

Now all I feel is guilt, so I hastily pull the gum out of my pocket and place it back on the shelf before a security camera sees me, or worse: Annie.

Annie skips out of the bathroom and eyes the candy selection hungrily.

"No," I say before she can ask, but of course she asks anyway.

We walk back to the car with two bags full of snacks, none of them stolen.

By some miracle, I sleep for a few more hours. The rest of the trip is a blur of driving and bathroom breaks and fast food, and a phone call from my hyper girlfriend who apparently just found out I'm moving.

"Listen, Liv... it wasn't working anyway," I tell her.

She's yelling and cursing and crying on her end of the line about how awful I am and how I could never make a girl happy. Eventually I just hang up and go back to sleep.

Finally we pass the big green sign with white lettering that says: *Welcome to Kentucky, the Bluegrass State.*

"How much longer?" Annie mumbles sleepily.

Outside my window I see the sloping plains of the countryside sitting beneath a starry blue sky, and I have to admit: It's beautiful.

"It isn't too far," Mom promises. "Why don't you go to sleep?"

By the sound of her soft breathing, it seems Annie has.

Mom and I sit in silence, and I can hear the frogs peeping and owls calling to each other. The sound of a lone coyote howling to a friend in the distance sends chills up my spine, but not the nervous kind. A strange curiosity rises inside of me as I open my eyes to this world I've never known, and I don't even mind the reek of manure that burns in my nose.

I'm probably just tired, but right now the move seems like what Jackson suggested it was: A new opportunity. For a new home, a new life, new friendships...

It's barely been ten minutes before Mom pulls the car into the driveway of a small white house. It doesn't have much of a field, but I think that the forest is part of Grandma's land. I look at the tall, black silhouettes of the trees behind the house, and I realize that the forest extends past Grandma's property and into another.

The neighboring house on the right side is a bit smaller, but there's much more land. I can also make out the shape of a horse standing near the edge of its pasture, gazing at me as if it's welcoming us home.

Because that's what it feels like, somehow. It feels like home.

. . .

Grandma embraces us one by one, laughing and crying at the same time. She looks good for her age, with dark brown hair (obviously dyed, but still), a nice smile and bright green eyes like mine.

"I'm so happy you're all coming to stay with me," she says when she's hugging Mom. "You don't know how lonely it's been around here, without your father..." She takes a deep breath and forces a smile. "I'm sure you're all exhausted after that drive, so you'll probably want to wait to unpack until tomorrow, but your boxes and everything are in my sunroom for when you're ready. If you're hungry, I have tea and snacks in the kitchen... oh, and coffee for you, Margaret." She adds to Mom with a knowing smile.

We follow Grandma into the kitchen, which looks exactly like I would have pictured it. It's rustic-looking and quaint, with a black and white tiled floor and a little island in the center. There are decorations with roosters and some other farm animals, including the salt and pepper shakers, a sign that says 'Farm Kitchen' and a stack of coasters.

"So, tell me about the trip," Grandma says, addressing no one in particular.

I sit at a stool beside the island, followed by a drowsy-looking Annie. Mom heads to the counter to pour some coffee for herself, which seems pretty pointless considering the fact that she's about to go to sleep.

"It was long," I say when no one else says anything, and Grandma laughs.

"I thought as much," she says, sitting across from us. "So tell me, Malcolm. You got yourself a girlfriend?"

I feel like I should be uncomfortable, but I guess I'm too tired. "Nope," I say shortly.
"Well, that's good," she says, catching me off-guard. "Because there's a pretty girl next door who's about your age-"

Mom laughs, and now I do feel uncomfortable.

"I think I'm gonna hit the hay," I say as a little farm joke, and even Annie grins.

"Your room is up the stairs on the right," Grandma says with a warm smile. "It isn't much, but I think you'll like it. There's a... nice view."

"Thanks, Grandma." I gulp down the rest of my tea, before adding, "Goodnight."

Then I'm charging up the stairs as quickly as my feet will allow. I open the first door on my right, and I'm relieved to find that it's pretty average looking. It's about the size of my old room, with a small bed in the corner on the right, a dresser and a window covered by crimson curtains. Upon closer inspection, I realize that it isn't a window, but the door to a balcony.

I pull back the curtains and slide the glass door open, letting the warm, humid air meet me as I step out into the night. The sky is lit up by so many stars that it looks almost like day. I can see the forest and the neighbor's yard, where I spot the horse that I saw when we pulled in.

He tosses his mane and trots to the fence closest to me, gazing up and eyeing me curiously. I wonder how he knows I'm here.

Chapter Three

I sleep in much longer than usual. I don't know if it's the drive or this surprisingly comfortable mattress, but when I head down to the kitchen I learn that everyone else has been awake for a few hours already.

Grandma has pancakes, bacon and toast ready, and she asks Annie to go out to the chicken coop for some more eggs. Annie is eager to do it, but I have a feeling that the chore will get old to her soon enough.

Mom pulls me toward her for a hug, and I don't dodge her the way I normally do. I want her to be happy, and I want me to be happy. The best way to keep up the mutual happiness is by being as well-mannered as possible. In other words, I have to be Jackson.

"How'd you sleep?" I ask when she lets go. Mom is almost two inches shorter than I am now (I inherited my Dad's height) so I have to look down when I'm talking to her. Annie's head reaches the center of my chest, and Grandma probably stands to my shoulders.

"Very well," Mom says. "How about you?"

I flash her one of my hard-to-come-by genuine smiles. "Like a log."

When Annie returns, she hands Grandma the egg basket and beams. "I got six eggs."

"Good job, Annabel!" Grandma says, looking equally pleased. "I'm happy I've got one little farm helper here. How about you, Malcolm?"

I look up from my food and my eyes widen involuntarily. "Uh. What?"

Mom laughs. "Are you going to help out with farm work?"

I frown, feeling as if I've been tricked into something and didn't realize until now. Then I force a smile, because I need to be cooperative. "Of course I'll help if you... uh... need me to."

Mom's phone starts buzzing and she fishes it out of her purse.

We have service here? I think in amazement.

"Hello?" Mom says into the phone. "Oh, Frank. Yes, yes... we're out. Mm-hm. We're at my mother's house. Yes, I took the offer. No, the kids are fine. Of course I would tell you if something happened." She rolls her eyes, and makes the 'crazy' gesture with her finger to Annie. "Okay, yeah... that's fine. Yes. Um... I don't think you should talk to him right now. No, I'm not keeping him from you, Frank, I'm just..." Mom sighs and turns to look at me. "Do you want to talk to your father?"

I shake my head quickly, shoveling a forkful of pancake into my mouth just in case I need an excuse.

"He doesn't want to talk right now," Mom says wearily, like she's trying to calm down an angry two-year-old. "Yes, I'll have him call you if he wants to. He's sixteen, Frank. He can make his own choices. No, I'm not saying they don't have any rules..." She leaves the room, and I have a feeling that Dad is going to make it a long conversation.

"I want to go see the horse," Annie remarks once she's put her plate in the sink. "The neighbor's horse. What's its name, Grandma?"

Grandma smiles, but her eyes are on mine instead of Annie's. "Maybe you two should go ask the horse's owner. She's a fresh breath of air, that girl. Sweet, smart..."

"We should probably unpack," I say quickly, clearing my plate. "Maybe another time. And I wouldn't want to bother her."

"I want to go see the horse *now*!" Annie cries.

"You don't get whatever you want, especially by crying and ordering people around," I tell her in a low voice.

Mom comes back into the kitchen and puts her phone on the counter. She looks exhausted, and I feel a burst of anger at my father for breaking her happiness.

"Malcolm, please take your sister outside," she says quietly. "I'll work on unpacking. I think you could both use the fresh air."

I open my mouth, but no sound comes out.

"See?" Annie sneers. "Let's go, Mal. I want to see the horse!" She trots off into the other room to get her shoes on, and I'm forced to follow.

"You're a little monster, you know that?" I ask under my breath.

Annie smiles. "Well obviously being a monster gets me what I want more than whatever you are," she says simply, and I have to give her credit. That was a good comeback- for an eight-year-old.

It's warmer than it was last night, and the sun has repossessed the vast sky that's no longer full of glittering stars. Annie goes straight toward the fence, and I know that I can't stop her. I follow, hoping to God that the girl doesn't come out while we're looking at her horse. I can already imagine the scenario:

Girl: *Why are you touching my horse?*

Me: *Sorry, my little sister is obsessed with horses and since she's a diva I'm forced to do whatever she wants.*

Girl: *Well that's pathetic.*

Me: *Trust me, I know. Oh, by the way, I know we've never met before... but my Grandmother seems to be trying to pair the two of us up, so watch out.*

She'd probably be more polite, but I don't want to take any chances. I keep an eye out for any sign of other people, but it's only Annie and I. The horse meets us at the wire fence where we stand, his magnificent black mane tossing behind him as he moves. His eyes are dark brown and watchful, framed by long brown eyelashes that catch the sunlight and gleam.

"She's so beautiful," Annie says quietly, looking up at the horse in awe.

"It's a stallion, actually."

"A stallion?" Annie repeats. "Is that a kind of horse?"

"It means it's a boy."

Annie glares at me. "How would you know it's a boy? You won't talk to the owner like Grandma said because you're afraid."

I roll my eyes. "I just know, okay Annie? I think that's enough for today. You've seen it, now we can go inside."

"I want to ask the owner if I can ride him."

"No way. Even if she said you could, stallions can be dangerous. You're too small," I say quickly.

Annie's eyebrows tighten and she squints her eyes, and her face literally starts turning red. She's a maniac devil child if ever there was one.

"I'm telling Mom," she threatens.

"What, that I won't let you do something dangerous? That the owner isn't here to ask? That you're the biggest brat on the planet?"

"Jerk!" Annie cries, and runs toward the house crying.

I let out a big, tired breath and look back at the horse. He still stands beside the fence, his ears pricked forward and his eyes thoughtful.

"Have you ever had a sister, boy?" I whisper, running my hand up his muzzle. He makes a small sound in his throat that I take as agreement, and I smile. "Good boy. What's your name, huh?"

I jump at the sound of an engine starting, and the stallion and I both try to locate the source.

Further into the neighbor's yard I see a girl. She's sitting on a mud-splattered, army green quad with a trailer attached to the back. She stops it at an open-air shed and puts the quad into neutral, before hopping off and loading the back with hay. Her hair falls in brown waves that reach the end of her torso.

I'm too busy watching her to think about her seeing me petting her horse, and I only come to my senses once she's gotten back on the quad and starts driving in this direction.

I turn around and race back to the house, hoping that she didn't catch a glimpse of a blonde city kid talking to her horse and then racing off because he was too much of a wimp to introduce himself.

- - -

The day mostly consists of unpacking, Annie complaining about me, and more unpacking. I try to keep calm and happy for Mom, but Brat Kid is getting on my nerves.

Grandma makes stew for dinner, with freshly baked bread that tastes like it was made in Heaven itself.

"This is delicious, Grandma."

Grandma beams. "Thank you, Malcolm. Maybe while you're staying here I can teach you some of my famous cooking tricks."

"Sounds good to me." Mom's phone is buzzing again, so I say, "Mom, just don't answer it."

She answers it anyway, and Grandma gives her a disapproving look.

"Hey, Frank," Mom says into the phone. Her eyebrows furrow after a moment, and I can hear that Dad is talking quickly on the other line. I can't make out the words he's saying, but he sounds pretty upset. "Slow down," Mom tells him. "Frank, what did they say?" She's quiet for a few moments, and the color drains from her face. "Are they... completely sure?" I can make out the words 'body' and 'looking now' on the other line.

Mom's hand flies to her mouth and she lets out a choked sob. She rises from the table, and hangs up the phone without saying goodbye. Then she just crumples like a rag doll, falling back into her chair and putting her head in her hands.

"What's wrong?" I ask, and my voice doesn't sound familiar. I feel that lack of control again, and it's terrifying.

Mom doesn't stop crying until her tears run dry. We've moved into the living room, and the three of us surround her and try to comfort her. The problem is, we don't have any idea what's wrong. I consider calling Dad to find out, but if it's my business Mom will tell me directly.

Finally she speaks, her face as white as paper and her lips quivering. "It's Jackson."

It's all she needs to say.

Chapter Four

I think that days might pass by without me knowing it, because I can recall many different meals being brought to me and visits from my Mom, Grandma and even Annie trying to convince me to leave my room.

But I can't. Every time I remember that Jackson is dead, another wave of panic and pain rushes over me.

One day, Mom comes into the room and sits down at the end of my bed. She doesn't say anything for a little while, and neither do I.

When she does speak, her voice is hollow. "The funeral is the day after tomorrow. You don't have to come if you don't want to, but… I think you'll regret it if you don't." She sits silently for a few more moments, before adding, "Think about it. If you don't want to go I understand, but I'd prefer if you weren't here by yourself."

I roll over to face the wall, hoping that Mom will get the message.

"Okay," Mom whispers.

Then she leaves.

The only visitor who I acknowledge is Annie, who comes to talk to me when they get back from the funeral. She describes the ceremony, telling me about the soldier's flag folding ritual that made Mom cry. She talks about all of the people who attended, from old family friends to distant relatives we haven't seen in years.

"You know who wasn't there, though?" Annie asks curiously, as if she and I are actually having a conversation. "Lily. Do you think she and Jackson broke up before he died?"

My stomach tightens, and I say the first thing I've said in days. "It was probably too long of a drive."

Annie's quiet for a few moments, before, "Do you think they would have gotten married? I mean, she did love him, didn't she?"

I don't bother responding.

- - -

I feel like I'm in the dark, and my feet keep taking me down the wrong paths that are actually dead-ends. It's like a maze, and I'm wandering through it alone.

The thing that brings me out of the dark is a dream. A dream that I know I've had before, weeks ago when I still lived in Massachusetts.

"You need to be there for Mom and Annie," Jackson told me. *"I love them so much, and so do you, even if you forget it sometimes. I know you're upset, but*

32

you have to remember... you're all they have. And you can keep them safe.

"Life will keep coming at you, Mal. It'll seem hopeless. Whatever happens, you need to stick through it. You need to fight back."

So today is the day that I do fight back. I get out of bed for the first time this week (not including any trips to the bathroom) and head downstairs. Mom and Grandma are standing in the kitchen talking, but they go quiet when they see me.

Mom comes over and gives me a big hug, which is probably just as much to comfort her as it to comfort me. I force myself to hug her back, even though I feel numb and it's hard to make my limbs move.

"I'm so glad you're up, Mal," she whispers. "You scared us."

I open my mouth to say I'm sorry, but I realize that I'm not. I wasn't in control. When I found out about Jackson, the darkness took over and all I could do was stay still and let it happen.

She pulls back and holds my shoulders, looking between my eyes dolefully. "Are you okay, honey?"

No, I'm not okay. My favorite person in the entire world, the only person I could truly rely on, is dead. He's not dead for a week. Not a month, not even a few years. Death is forever. I have to live the rest of my life without him.

I don't tell her all of this. I just say, "I'm fine."

. . .

Maybe I'm out of bed, but the darkness doesn't go away. It feels like my head is full of fog and I can't think straight, and my actions are based off of instinct rather than thought. I feel more like I'm watching my life than actually living it.

Of course the others are depressed about Jackson's death, but suddenly they seem to be more worried about me. Mom watches me from the corner of her eye whenever we're in the same room as if I won't notice, but of course I do. It just makes me feel worse now that everyone is being so careful around me.

Finally the day comes when Mom says, "Malcolm, it's time for you to start seeing someone."

At first I don't know what she means. For a moment I think she's talking about a girlfriend, as in 'seeing someone' seeing someone, but then I understand what she means.

"Mom," I say, gaping at her. "You want me to see a shrink?"

"A therapist, honey," Mom says gently. "And only for a little while. They can help you to get better."

"But I'm fine," I lie.

"No, you're not," Mom says, and her eyes are suddenly brimming with tears. "You're not fine. You've been acting so dead recently."

I flinch at the word.

Dead. Dead like Jackson.

"All you'd have to do is talk to him. If you go once and don't like it, I won't ask you to do it again. Please, Malcolm," she pleads, and I can see the pain in her eyes.

I can almost hear Jackson's voice in my head. *"I know you're upset, but you have to remember... you're all they have. And you can keep them safe."*

My shoulders slump. "Okay, Mom."

Mom gives me a hug. "Everything will get better. I promise."

I give her a weak smile. "I hope so."

. . .

Mom drops me off the following day at ten o'clock, and I walk into the building with my hands in my pockets. I might seem calm and confident to onlookers, but inside I'm trembling. The coward inside of me wants to turn around and run back to the car, but I force my feet to keep moving forward.

I almost wish I had let Mom walk me in. When she offered I refused, saying that I must be pretty pathetic if I can't walk myself into my own appointment.

I shouldn't be here, I think as I approach the front desk. I'm surprised that even in a small town like this there would be a counselor's office.

I sort of wish there wasn't.

The lobbyist smiles at me, that fake smile people wear in customer service. "Do you have an appointment?" she asks in a sugary voice.

I nod.

She turns to her computer and places her fingers on the keyboard. "Name, please."

"Malcolm Gibbs," I say, and it sounds almost like a question.

She types it in and studies the screen. "Take a seat over there, please. Dr. Waterman will be right with you."

I thank her, and then head to the row of chairs to sit down. I pick the one furthest from the corner, because if someone else sits I'll be locked in.
I feel insecure even after I sit down, looking around the room and wishing again that Mom was with me. I pull out my phone and check the time, even though I've been in the building for only about a minute.

"Malcolm Gibbs?"

I look up in surprise, and see a man that must be Dr. Waterman standing on the other side of the room with a clipboard. He seems friendly enough, with bright eyes and warm brown skin. His hair is curly and black, and is shaved down so it's only stubble on the top of his head.

I stand up hesitantly and follow him down a short hall. We turn into one of the first rooms, and I'm relieved that it isn't like the exam rooms at doctors offices. I close the door behind me and sit in the chair across from Dr. Waterman, who's looking down at his clipboard thoughtfully.

"So you're new to town," he says.

"Word travels that quickly around here?"

Waterman laughs. "It's a small town. I just thought I would have recognized you if I'd seen you before."

"Oh. So... uh... I should call you Dr. Waterman?" I ask, feeling like an idiot.

"You can call me whatever you want," he says with a grin. "Superman, King Kong..." He gets a smile out of me. "My first name is Samuel."

"Sam, then?"

"That's what most people call me," he replies with a nod.

I'm surprised by Samuel Waterman. I thought therapists were formal, and they only talked about you and your problems. Sam makes me feel comfortable, and he tells me things about him. Maybe this isn't so bad, after all.

"So," Sam says, his smile falling away a bit, and I know that we've gotten to that point of the conversation. "Tell me what's been going on."

I take a deep breath and look down at my hands. "Well, a lot's been going on. I don't know where to start."

Sam thinks for a few moments. "Can you tell me about your family?"

"My Mom is an insurance adjuster. Annie is my little sister, and she's the most annoying person I've ever met- and I'm not just saying that because she's my sister," I say sullenly. Now that I've started talking I can't seem to make myself stop. "Mom got a job offer here last month and didn't think she'd be able to take it. My Dad didn't want to move, but then, he doesn't do much of anything. He's lazy and rude and thinks other people owe him something..." I hesitate for a moment before adding, "He's an alcoholic."

Sam doesn't speak, he only listens and writes a few things down on his clipboard.

"Finally Mom decided to get a divorce, and she accepted the job offer here in Kentucky. We moved in with my grandmother... she's been living alone since Grandpa died last year. And now..." I trail off, thinking again about the reason I'm here. "It was already a lot to handle, but a week ago I really thought I could do it. And then Mom got the call. My older brother, Jackson..." I make myself stop for a moment, because my voice trembles and I'm afraid I'm going to start crying. I close my eyes and force myself to take steady breaths. "Jackson is... was... in the army. He died last week."

"I'm so sorry," Sam says with genuine sincerity. "Were you and your brother close?"

"Yes," I say quietly. "He was my best friend. The only one I trusted completely. I mean, I trust my mom, but..." I trail off, not knowing how to finish.

Sam leans back in his chair, studying me. He looks down at his clipboard and sighs. "You definitely have a lot going on. I can see why you'd be feeling depressed. Someone your age shouldn't need to deal with so much stress, but unfortunately unfair things like that are a big part of life. You can't control it."

You're telling me what I already know, I think miserably.

"But there are some things you *can* control," Sam continues. "You can control how you react to those unfair things. What you do when you're under stress is a big part of who you are. For example, true leaders take control and don't let themselves be taken over by anxiety. What kind of person are you, Malcolm Gibbs?"

"I don't know."

"Then let's find out. I suggest you start keeping a log," Sam says. "Write about things you do every day, and how you feel. You'll most likely start to see improvement in your mood when you read back over the days. Next week when you come see me you can show me the log, or you can keep it to yourself. It's completely up to you."

I almost laugh. "You want me to keep a diary?"

"Of sorts," Sam replies, and I realize that he isn't joking. "You don't have to call it that, though. And you don't have to start each entry with 'dear diary.' I've had some people who address it to someone they love. A pet, a family member..."

"Jackson," I say. "I'll write it to Jackson."

Sam smiles. "Very good. So you'll come back next week?"

"I'll come back next week," I repeat.

Sam stands. "Thank you, Malcolm. I'm looking forward to it." I start toward the door, and he adds, "Remember that log."

I nod once before I leave the room.

Chapter Five

"How was it?" Mom asks once I've shut the car door behind me.

"It was good."

"So..."

"I'm going back next week," I finish for her. "That is, if it's okay."

"Of course it's okay!" Mom says, pleased. "What did you two talk about? Actually, never mind. It isn't my business. Oh, I'm so glad you're going back."

"Me too. And I need a notebook."

"We can stop and pick one up on the way home. You can look for one you like." She doesn't ask why I need it, and I'm grateful.

. . .

They don't have a large selection, but it doesn't need to be special. I pick up a black composition notebook, but I decide that I should find one that feels more like me. I don't want a blank black notebook to symbolize my life.

Most of the notebooks are colorful and decorated with pictures of kittens and donuts and witty sayings, but none feel right. I'm hoping for a leather one, or something simple but unique. Finally I find one that fits my liking. It's a five-by-eight journal with a hard brown cover and the word 'LIVE' in big white letters. I hold it against my chest and take a deep breath. Jackson would like this one.

I write in it for the first time after dinner. I go up to my room and sit on the balcony, and my only company is the black stallion that gazes up at me from his pasture. I lower the pencil to the paper and begin the entry.

Dear Jackson,

I know you'll never read this, but I still have to write it. Not just for Mom and Superman (A.K.A. Dr. Samuel Waterman), but also for me. What can I tell you about?
Oh yeah, Grandma wants me to 'get to know' this girl next door who I've never met before. I saw her feeding her horse the other day, but only from a distance. I haven't seen anyone else in this town except the ones I met when I went to go see Sam. Our little diva is back to Brat Kid mode, by the way. It's hard to be mature when she's around to irritate me, but I'm trying. I'll make you proud, I swear. If you're up there in that sky full of stars looking down on me, maybe send me some good luck? I could really use it right about now.

- Malcolm

. . .

I sleep peacefully tonight. It isn't the dark stupor I was in for the last week or two, but a feeling of elevation like I'm sleeping on a cloud way up in the sky. When I wake up the sun has barely risen, and when I go out on the balcony it looks like the golden yolk of a chicken egg was spilled across the horizon. I try to find my stallion friend in the semi-darkness, and I realize that he's standing right beside the fence. He isn't alone.

The girl sits in the grass beside him, making gestures with her hands as if she's talking to him. He stands over her protectively, and occasionally reaches his head down to nuzzle her. Under the light of dawn that lights up the stretching green field around them, it might be the most beautiful thing I've ever seen.

That's when the horse turns to look up at me the way he does whenever I'm watching him, and after a moment the girl follows his gaze. I consider leaving the balcony and pretending I haven't seen them, but what's the point?

I raise a hand in greeting and the girl mirrors the movement. We watch each other for a minute, as if waiting for the other person to do something. Finally I do. I turn around and walk back inside, closing the glass door behind me.

I walk down the stairs quietly, and of course no one is awake. I sit down in an armchair in the living room and sigh, wondering how crazy it would be if I went outside right now and talked to that girl. I've almost convinced myself to do it, to take control of my life and do something spontaneous, when Annie stumbles into the room.

"Oh, you're awake?" she asks when she sees me.

"No. I'm a figment of your imagination."

Annie sits down on the couch, rubbing her eyes sleepily. "You know, you don't always need to be sarcastic." She yawns. "Can we play outside?"

My stomach leaps at the thought of Annie running over to the stallion and me needing to talk to our neighbor. I guess it wouldn't be so bad, unless Annie embarrassed me... the most likely scenario.

"It's too early."

Annie crosses her arms over her chest, her eyebrows furrowed. "No it's not. That's just an excuse. You're afraid of seeing that girl."

"What girl?"

Annie rolls her eyes. "Like you don't know. I saw her out the window with her stallion, and I know you've seen her too. That's why you didn't want me by the horse. Grandma wants you two to get married," she adds, snickering.

"Shut up," I snap.

"So you'll take me outside?"

"No."

Annie stands without saying another words, and disappears from the room. I begin to feel uneasy; she never gives up when she wants something.

I begin to wonder if she went back to bed, when she calls, "I guess I'll have to take myself outside." The front door slams shut.

"Annie!" I growl, and hurry to get my shoes on.

. . .

Of course she's by the horse. Of course the horse is standing by the fence. Of course the girl is standing beside the horse standing by the fence.

She's talking to Annie, who is nodding and petting the horse. All three of them look up at my approach, and I try to look pleasant despite my burning hatred for my sister.

"Hey there," the girl says. She wears what you'd expect a country girl to wear, a button-up checkered blue and white shirt tucked into flare jeans. I expect to see cowgirl boots when I look to her feet, but they're just muck boots.

"Hey," I reply casually. At least, I hope I sound casual. Truthfully my heart is beating a hundred miles a minute. "I'm sorry about my sister. I told her not to mess with your horse."

"No, she's fine," the girl says quickly, flashing Annie a smile. "I'm happy to introduce Blue to other people."

"Blue?" I repeat. "Why Blue?"

"His full name is Blue Jeans," the girl explains. "Blue for short. I got him when I was five," she adds.

"So you can see why I'd name him something like that. It suits him, though."

"Hey, Blue," I say, reaching out and stroking his muzzle. Blue whinnies and pushes his head closer to me in what seems to be an affectionate gesture.

"He likes you," the girl says with a smile. "I've never seen him do that to a stranger."

"And he likes me too, right Bella?" Annie asks.

The girl- Bella, apparently- laughs. "Yes, he certainly does." Her eyes flit up to catch mine and she grins. She has the kind of smile you can't help but smile back to.

"I'm Malcolm."

She puts out a hand over the fence. "Isabel. Everyone calls me Bella."

I take her hand and shake it. "Nice to meet you, Bella."

"It's nice to meet you too."

Annie stands on her toes as if she feels the lack of attention toward her is due to her height. "Isn't it so cool that Bella and I almost have the same name? Isabel and Annabel."

"Very cool," I say, my thumbs in my pockets.

"Maybe we're sisters," Bella teases, giving Annie another smile.

This girl smiles a lot, I think, but I can't help liking it.

"That would mean Malcolm is your brother, too," Annie warns. "And he's a jerk."

"I'm not a jerk," I say quickly, heat rising to my face, but Bella is laughing.

Annie is pleased. "Can I ride Blue?"

"Sorry, Annie, but I have to go. I still haven't done my morning chores."

Annie frowns. "What are you doing now, then?"

Bella strokes Blue's fur absentmindedly. "I was just coming to check on Blue. I had a dream that he was... um... hurt. In an accident." I can tell by her hesitation that she said 'hurt' for Annie's sake. I'm sure what she meant was far worse.

Pain rips through my chest and my hand finds my heart automatically. It's mental, I know that. I wonder if it'll always hurt this way when people mention their loved ones dying. One part of me hopes that it does. That way I'll remember how much I love Jackson in case I begin to forget him.

The other part of me wishes that I didn't have to feel any pain at all.

"I'll come back when I'm done, though," Bella promises. "You know, it gets lonely around here. Now that you two live next door, you can come talk to me if you see me by the fence. It'd be nice to have some company."

"We will," Annie says eagerly.

Bella smiles, before leaving the pasture to do her chores.

Suddenly I feel pathetic for not having any chores to do.

"Now do you want to go inside, Annie?"

Annie considers this, and for a moment I actually think she might say yes. Then she jumps forward and touches my shoulder, shouting, "Tag!" She runs off giggling and I roll my eyes.

Alright, fine. I'll play the nice big brother for a while.

Annie scurries behind the chicken coop and I follow her, and soon we're running in circles around it and laughing.
I sneak around the opposite way, and when I hear Annie squeal in surprise I leap forward to tag her. She falls to the ground, giggling. It's only when she's pushed her hair out of her face that I see the blood streaming from her nose.

"Annie!" I exclaim, pulling her to her feet.

She's still laughing. "What?"

"Cover your nose, and whatever you do don't tilt your head back. We need to get inside and grab some paper towels," I say, pushing her toward the house.

Her eyebrows furrow in confusion, but she reaches up to her nose anyway. Her eyes widen when she feels the moisture, and pulls her hand away to look down at her bloodied fingers.

"Keep your hand there!" I insist, practically dragging her. "Try pinching the bridge of your nose."

I've never seen a nose bleed that much. Even when I've gotten her inside and handed her over to Mom it hasn't stopped bleeding. Even after they've been in the bathroom with a wad of paper towels for a full five minutes it hasn't stopped bleeding. I start getting worried, but eventually the bleeding stops and Annie's fine.

"I didn't even hit my nose," she tells Mom when we're all sitting in the living room. "I hit my head when I fell, but not my nose."

Mom looks to me. "Mal, did you see what happened?"

I swallow. "Annie and I were playing tag. I was chasing her," I say, and it seems stupid now. "When I scared her she fell backward onto the ground, but not very hard."

Annie's wringing her hands together nervously. "Is that... normal?"

Mom bites her lip. "You probably need some water, honey. And both of you need to be more careful."

"We will," I say quickly. Annie might be the most irritating kid on the planet, but she's still my little sister.

You love them, Mal, even if you forget it sometimes, Jackson reminds me.

I know, I think back. *And I'm trying harder to show them that. I promise.*

Chapter Six

"Malcolm, do you want to help your sister and I shuck corn?"

Grandma and Annie are sitting at the island with a heaping pile of corn cobs. The garbage can sits on the floor beside them so they can toss the shucks away when they're done.

"It's really fun," Annie urges.

I force a smile. "Thanks for the offer, but I'm going to go check out the barn. Mom says there might be an old basketball hoop in there."

Annie rolls her eyes. "You and basketball."

I decide to ignore her instead of making a witty comeback, though several come to mind.

"Be careful," Grandma warns. "There's some rusty old farm equipment in there. I hope you're up-to-date on your tetanus shots."

"I am," I assure her, though I don't actually know for sure. "And I'll be careful."

. . .

It looks like no one's been in the barn for years. The structure isn't very sound, with creaking floorboards and walls that seem to be caving in.

The roof definitely needs repairs as well. If it was raining, I might as well stand outside rather than in here.

I like it, though. It feels like something you'd see in a scary movie, an abandoned barn with old wood and strange storage laying around. Hay litters the floor, and a mouse runs across my feet while I'm searching.

The barn has three sections. There's the main area you see when you first walk in, a back room that looks almost like a large horse stall, and a loft. If I fixed this place up, maybe the loft could be mine. It's open-air (probably not intentionally) with a full view of the sky and forest.

I find the basketball hoop laying on the ground in the back room, covered with cobwebs and straw but all in one piece. It takes several minutes to pull it out of the barn, and then I worry about cleaning it off. I go above and beyond, bringing out a wet rag and wiping it down. I won't have a hoop of mine looking like it's been sitting in a barn for the past ten years, even though it probably has.

Grandma's driveway is my best bet for playing, so I bring it to the edge and stand it up. Finally I go inside and retrieve my basketball, and for a while I can forget all of the awful, unfair things that have been going on. It's just me and the ball. No death, no pain, no neglect. I dribble it for a while, pretending that I'm dodging opponents and passing to invisible teammates. I need to run around the ball to catch it when I become said teammates, and then I continue to the hoop and shoot. I play until my arms are sore, and then I just practice free throws.

"You're good," Bella observes. She's leaning back against a tree that stands at the edge of her yard.

I'm suddenly self-conscious of the sweat that's dripping down my face and shirt, but I push the feeling away. "Thanks. Do you play?"

Bella smiles. "A bit."

I toss her the ball, and step back to give her room. She walks over and looks up at the hoop, which is at least three feet above her head. She dribbles the ball a few times and then shoots. It falls through the hoop, sending the net swishing back and forth.

"Beginners luck," I say coolly, and she lifts an eyebrow.

"Oh yeah? I bet I could beat you one on one."

I shrug. "Only one way to find out."

Bella picks up the ball and tosses it to me, and we pass it back and forth to check it in. Then I start forward, the ball flying up and down beneath my hand as I try to round her.

She's quicker. Her arm flies out to hit the ball out of my hand, and in a moment she's dribbling the last few feet to the hoop and shooting it.

She catches it as it falls through the net, and turns to flash me a smile. "One point for me."

We play four more rounds, and Bella wins 3:2. At this point we're both sweating and breathing hard, and I'm clutching my stomach due to a painful dehydration cramp.

"I have to admit, you're pretty good," I say, sitting down in the grass at the edge of the driveway.

"Pretty good?"

"Okay, very good. Maybe even better than me."

Bella sits down a few feet away and smiles. "I guess the score speaks for itself."

I roll my eyes, but I'm grinning too.

"So, you're Mrs. Gibbs' grandson," Bella says.

It isn't a question, but I answer it anyway. "Yeah."

"Are you just staying for the summer?"

I shake my head. "We're probably staying for good."

Bella's quiet for a moment. Then, "How old are you?"

"Sixteen. You?"

"I'll be sixteen on July seventh," she says. "We're going to have a barbeque on the 4th, and my parents are calling it my birthday party. It's sort of annoying, considering they do a fourth of July barbeque every year." She thinks for a moment. "Hey, you should come. Annie, too. And your grandmother and parents."

"Yeah, that would be fun. But uh, not both parents. My Dad lives in Massachusetts, back at our old house. My parents just got divorced."

"Oh," Bella says quietly, her face flushed. "I'm sorry. I shouldn't have assumed-"

"No, it's fine. Thanks for inviting me. I'll tell my family about it and see if they want to go. I know for a fact that Annie will want to come."

Bella's smiling again. "Annie's adorable."

I laugh. "Oh Bella, if only you knew."

. . .

At dinner I try to find an opportunity to tell the others about Bella's barbeque. It should be easy.

I could just say: 'Hey, the neighbors invited me to a barbeque. Do you all want to come?'

Maybe the reason I don't want to say it is because Grandma and Annie will most likely tease me about it, and Mom will give me that knowing smile that makes me want to tear out my eyebrows.

"Are we doing anything on Friday?" I venture.

"No. Why?" Mom asks, surprised.

"Well..." *Just say it. Rip off the band aid.* "Our neighbor, Bella, invited us all to go to her family's fourth of July barbeque."

Annie squeals. "Can we, Mom?"

Grandma only grins.

"I don't see why not," Mom says after a moment. "It was nice of her to invite us. Do you know what time?" She doesn't ask when I talked to Bella.

I shake my head. "No, but I can find out."

Grandma smiles for the rest of dinner.

. . .

Dear Jackson,

Thanks for the good luck. Everything's getting better... I hope. I found Grandpa's old basketball hoop and played for a while. The girl's name is Bella. We're going to her house on Friday for a barbeque. I'm not sure if I should bring a present- considering I've only talked to her twice and know almost nothing about her- but I think I'll do it anyway. I have an idea in mind.

Until next time,

- Malcolm

Chapter Seven

It takes about an hour of searching in the barn this morning, but I find it. A worn out basketball that, with a bit of cleaning up, will hopefully look as good as new. I wipe it down with a moistened paper towel when I get inside, but it still doesn't look as good as mine. I decide to give Bella mine, instead.

She probably has her own, which is why I need to make this one special. I rip a piece of paper out of my journal and sketch different designs I could write on its surface, but none seem to fit her personality. At least, not the personality I've seen in the short time I've known her.

Bella is bright and friendly, but also competitive. Her smile is contagious, her eyes are the kind you can't look away from...

I freeze, shocked by the change in my thoughts. *Why am I thinking of her this way? I barely know her. Anyway, she's just a friend. Maybe she's not even that. She's just a... neighbor. A neighbor with a really beautiful smile.* I shake my head. *Focus. Just make a pattern that she'll like and write her name. No big deal.*

I end up writing her name in big, 3D-looking font with colorful sharpies I stole from Annie's room.

Around her name I sketch pictures of horses and vines that weave in intricate patterns around the ball, and after an hour or two I'm finished.

Maybe I don't know Bella very well, but I do know that she'll love this.

I hide it under my bed so no one will ask me about it, before heading downstairs. Mom looks up at my approach, her computer on her lap. She's sitting on the couch with a clipboard, writing down phone numbers and notes and whatever else she does for her job.

All I really know about it is that she has to talk to people on the phone all day and sometimes go out and inspect car and property damage, which really has no appeal to me.

"Have you seen Annie this morning?" she asks.

"No. She's probably sleeping."

Mom looks down at her watch, and then back up at me. "It's almost eleven. Will you go check on her?"

Back up the stairs I go.

Annie is laying in her bed, and the moment I see her I know that something's off. Her lips are trembling and beads of sweat are dripping down her forehead. Her blankets are pulled up to her chin, though it must be eighty degrees in here.

"Hey, Annie," I say, nudging her shoulder.

A round of shivers takes over her body and her eyes fly open. "Jackson?"

My stomach clenches. "No, Malcolm. Are you feeling okay?"

Annie's eyes close again and she pulls the blanket to her nose. "My belly hurts," she whispers.

I reach out and touch her forehead, and instantly draw my hand away. "I'll be right back," I say gently, and hurry to go get Mom.

- - -

The three of us sit in the waiting room at the doctor's office. Annie is laying her head against Mom's chest and whimpering. I fiddle with my phone, but I'm not actually concentrating on what I'm doing. All I can think about is all of the things that could be wrong with Annie.

It's not a big deal, I think hurriedly. It's probably the flu.

"Annabel Gibbs?" The nurse says from the doorway.

Mom stands, and Annie follows shakily.

"Do you want me to wait here?" I ask them.

"No," Annie mumbles, reaching out for me. I take her hand, which is warm despite the medicine Mom gave her for her fever.

The nurse leads us to an exam room, and I lift Annie onto the table. She sits and rubs her eyes drowsily, and I wonder if she might fall asleep before the doctor comes in. The nurse asks Mom a few questions and then leaves, and the doctor arrives five minutes later.

"So, Annie, how have you been feeling today?" The doctor asks.

Oh, she's been feeling wonderful. In perfect health, too. We're here for small talk.

"I feel sick," Annie says quietly.

"Can you tell me what hurts?"

Annie thinks for a moment. "My belly hurts a lot, and my head does too. Mostly my ear."

"Which ear, sweety?"

Annie points to her left ear, and the doctor peers inside with an otoscope. After a moment she removes it and says, "It's pretty swollen in there. I believe Annie has an inner ear infection, but I'm going to need to ask you a few more questions." She sits down with her laptop and types something in. "How has Annie's diet been?"

"She's a good eater," Mom says. "Not at all picky. We tend to eat fruits and vegetables for snacks, and she likes to drink milk."

The doctor nods and types it into her computer. "Has she complained about her ear before?"

"No."

"Has she experienced any headaches, bleeding or other injuries within the past two weeks?"

Mom and I exchange a look. "She did have a bad nosebleed yesterday," Mom says hesitantly.

The doctor nods again. "That can be common when children have ear infections, as can stomachaches like the one she's complained about. We can give her an antibiotic..."

Mom and the doctor continue their discussion, but my focus is on Annie.

You gave me a good scare, kid, I think.

If something were to happen to Annie... I'll have lost both of my siblings. I don't think I'd be able to handle it.

- - -

By this afternoon, Annie is back to her usual self. I help Grandma set the table, and we all sit down to eat. It's nice not needing to worry about something being wrong. I feel like I've been on the edge of my seat recently, like any unexpected problem could launch itself at me and wreck my artificial peace. Right now I'm letting myself relax.

"How are you feeling, Annie?" Grandma asks her.

"Much better," Annie says, handing her plate to Mom so she can serve her. She turns to look at me. "Were you worried about me, Malcolm?"

"Well I did go into the doctor's office with you, didn't I?"

"So you did worry about me?" Annie persists.

"Yes," I say, rolling my eyes. "I did."

"I'd worry about you, too," Annie says, taking her plate back from Mom. "Who would call me a brat if you weren't around?"

"And who would be a brat if you weren't around?" I retort.

Mom sighs. "Sibling love."

- - -

Dear Jackson,

Annie has an ear infection. This morning when I saw her, I swear I thought she was dying. I've never seen her like that. So vulnerable and frail-looking. I never want her to be like that again. Of course, now that she's had medicine she's acting like her good old self again (you know, like a spoiled little princess?). Tomorrow's Friday. I hope Bella likes her gift.

Talk to you tomorrow,

- Malcolm

Chapter Eight

Mom thinks we should be sophisticated and drive over instead of walking, which is perfectly fine with me. Bella's backyard is decorated with colorful streamers and picnic tables. One has been set with snacks and pitchers of drinks, as well as paper cups and plates.

At first I don't see Bella anywhere. Annie goes off to say hi to Blue, Mom and Grandma start talking to Bella's parents, and I stand against their house scanning the area. I hold the basketball under my arm, feeling self-conscious just standing here. I consider going back home, but then I see her.

Bella is wearing a knee-length jean skirt and a red white and blue top. Her hair is in two braids down her back, and she wears sandals that make her seem taller. When she spots me she smiles and jogs over.

"You came," she says, out of breath. Her cheeks are bright red from the heat, or maybe running around. She seems pretty energetic.

"I did. And I brought you this." I hand her the basketball, and she looks down at it with amazement. "I didn't know if I should bring you something, but I wanted to. It was mine... the one we played with the other day?"

"I love it!" Bella exclaims, turning the ball over in her hands and tracing the designs with her fingers. "Thank you."

"Now you can come over and practice with me whenever you want. But prepare to lose."

"In your dreams," Bella laughs. She sets the ball down on a picnic table, and asks, "Can I show you something?"

"Sure. Can I ask what it is?"

She grins mischievously. "You're going to have to trust me." She turns around and starts off, and I can't do anything but follow.

She leads me around a small orchard, through some clusters of willow trees, and we arrive at a log bridge that stretches over a wide stream. It isn't stagnant, but it's not moving very quickly, either. Bella sits down on the log and starts removing her sandals, and I just watch.

"Well?" she says, looking up at me.

"Well... what?"

"Don't you want to swim?"

My eyes widen involuntarily. Once I've recomposed my features I hold up my arms. "I'm not wearing swimming clothes."

She laughs. "Swimming clothes? You're not in Massachusetts anymore, city-boy."

She hops down from the bridge and into the steady stream of water, before laying back and letting it hold her afloat. She closes her eyes, and the sun lights up her face.

"Are you coming in?" She asks without opening her eyes.

I hesitate.

Take control, you wimp. You don't need to stick to routine. You don't need to stick to the rules. You need to be spontaneous.

"Why not?" I ask, and leap into the water.

It's warm, and reaches just above my waist. "Are you sure there aren't any leeches in here?"

Bella stands up. "I never said that." She laughs when she sees my shocked expression. "So, are you afraid to get wet?" She plunges under the water, and I look around to try and find her.

I gasp as something grabs hold of my foot, and a moment later I'm under water, too. I push off the ground and my head breaks the surface again. I'm breathing quickly, my eyes wide and my hair dripping wet.

Bella's having a laughing fit.

"Yeah, yeah, you're hilarious," I say, trying to wipe the water out of my eyes. I blink them open, and when I meet Bella's face I can't help smiling.

"We can look for crayfish, if you want," Bella suggests.

I begin to search the murky water uneasily as I recall the disgusting, crab-like creatures that apparently occupy this stream. "What would we do if we found them?"

Bella shrugs and starts searching. "I either let them go, or if I'm feeling creative I use them as bait."

"Bait for what?"

Bella looks at me like I know nothing. "Fishing?"

"Oh."

Bella gasps. "Oh, I see one!" She leans forward, and a moment later she holds it up by its torso. It wriggles in her fingers, and she beams like a kid on Christmas. "Want to hold it?"

"I'm good," I assure her. "Thanks, though."

Bella releases the crayfish and finds two more (or perhaps the same one multiple times) before we decide to head back.

"Where were you?" Mom asks, eyeing my soaked clothes with surprise.

Bella and I exchange a small smile, and I say, "Just exploring leech territory."

Mom looks from Bella to me, then shakes her head in that 'kids nowadays' kind of way. "Do you know where Annie went?"

"Last I saw her she was going to see Blue," I say. "Bella's horse."

"We can see if she's still over there," Bella offers.

"That would be nice of you," Mom says. "Thank you."

Bella and I head into the field and toward Blue's pasture, where Annie's standing and feeding him handfuls of grass.

"Hey, Annie," Bella says when we approach. "How's my favorite horse doing?"

"Isn't he your only horse?"

Bella laughs. "Yes, but he's still my favorite. I've met a lot of horses in my day."

I grin. "I've never heard someone under the age of sixty say that. 'In my day.'"

"Well it's true," Bella says, her eyes gleaming.

"Hamburgers are ready!" Bella's dad calls.

"Come on, Annie," I say, motioning toward the house with my head. "Want a piggyback ride?"

Maybe it's just the heat, but I feel strangely giddy.

"You're all wet, though!" she squeals.

"I didn't know you were afraid of water," I say in mock surprise.

Annie laughs and climbs onto my back, and I charge toward the house. Bella follows, and after a moment she's ahead of me. Suddenly it's a race between the two of us, and Annie is bumping around and laughing on my back. Bella reaches the picnic tables first, and Annie and I arrive a few seconds later. All three of us are laughing, and the people around us are looking over to see what's so funny.

Annie and I sit on one side of our table and Bella across from us, burgers and ice cold drinks in hand. We mostly talk about unimportant things, like who's better at basketball and the difference between country people and city people.

"I wish I looked like you, Bella," Annie says during a break in the conversation.

"Why? You're beautiful, Annie. I wish I had your hair," Bella replies.

"But your eyes are so pretty!" Annie insists. "And your hair is much longer than mine is. And-"

"What is it with girls and comparing their looks?" I ask, taking a big bite of my burger.

"What is it with boys and-" Annie starts, but Bella's mom calls out, 'Who wants to do sparklers?' and she forgets whatever she was going to say.

"Sparklers!" Annie cheers, leaping from her seat.

"Annie, finish your... food." She's already run off.

Bella laughs. "So full of energy. I miss being that small." She sighs and rests her head on her hand.

I think for a moment. "Do you go to the school here in town? Not now, obviously. During the school year." *What an idiot.*

"I'm homeschooled. Well, I was. I just graduated."

I lift my eyebrows. "You graduated?"

"I started kindergarten when I was three," she explains. "I've always been ahead. I'm probably going to the local university for my associates in the fall, but I don't know. I applied to a few other places, too."

"Wow," I say, leaning back and looking at her sideways. "I don't even know if I'm going to college."

"You should," Bella encourages. "You could probably get a sports scholarship. At least a partial one."

"Maybe."

The younger kids are running around with sparklers (dangerous, but why spoil their fun?), and Bella and I sit watching them for a while. The adults are conversing a few yards away, drinks in hand.

"I'm happy you moved in, Malcolm," Bella says, and I turn to look at her. She doesn't look nervous; her eyes are locked on mine as she waits for me to respond.

"So am I."

- - -

It starts to get dark, and the adults prepare fireworks. Bella and I sit on a picnic blanket in the grass looking up at the sky, where stars are beginning to take their places and the moon is shining brightest of all.

Bella sighs and lays back, her eyes shining under the light of the starry evening sky. I avert my gaze and watch as the first round of fireworks is set off. The children run around barefoot, screaming and cheering at the colorful sparks that explode in the sky.

"This is nice," I say quietly, and for the first time in a long time, I feel at peace.

"It is," Bella whispers, and she hesitantly slides her hand into mine. When she looks up at me, her smile is more spectacular than any fireworks. I can't seem to look away from her eyes, which flash between a million different colors...

The kids are screaming again, but this time their tone alarms me. Bella sits up suddenly and we both peer through the darkness to see the cause of the commotion.

Annie is on her hands and knees, and it takes me a moment to realize that she's vomiting. I jump to my feet and run over to her, pulling her hair away from her neck and wincing at the sound of her retching.

"Mom!" I call.

She doesn't hear me, but Bella's already on it. She hurries over and says something to Mom, before pointing at Annie and I.

Mom takes over holding Annie's hair back, and Grandma goes to start the car. I stand helplessly in the semi-darkness, plugging my ears to block out the explosions of fireworks that barely cover Annie's cries.

Why is it that whenever the world seems good, something happens to ruin the peace?

"I guess you're leaving, then?" Bella asks from behind me.

I turn and give her a sad smile. "Yeah."

"I hope Annie feels better," Bella says quietly.

"Me too."

I hold Bella's gaze for a few more seconds, and neither one of us says anything.

"Malcolm, let's go!" Mom calls from the car. She's helping Annie into her seat, and holding a grocery bag just in case she needs to be sick again.

"I'll see you soon," I promise.

"Here, put your number in," Bella says, handing me her phone. "That way you can give me updates."

I punch my number in. "Here you go. We'll talk later, okay?" I hurry to the car, my hands over my ears so I won't be sick, too.

Chapter Nine

Annie is sick all through the night, and late into the morning. She refuses to eat at breakfast, and eventually Mom says, "Enough is enough. We're going to the hospital."

"Do you want me to come?" I ask, petting Annie's head like she's a sick blonde puppy.

"You don't have to," Mom says, sliding her shoes on. "You can stay here with your grandmother."

"I want Malcolm to come," Annie whimpers.

"Then I will," I say gently, taking Annie's hand. "Come on, Annie. Let's get your shoes on, okay?"

Annie stumbles into her shoes, and I carry her to the car. The hospital is nearly half an hour away, and I'm relieved that Annie doesn't throw up again. I don't see how she could; there's probably nothing left in her stomach.

The doctors run a few tests, and I mostly sit on my phone in the corner of the room. Bella texts me and asks how Annie's doing.

Malcolm: At the hospital. They're running some tests

Bella: Do they have any idea what's wrong with her?

Malcolm: Haven't heard anything yet

Bella: Keep me posted, okay?

Malcolm: I will. Thanks Bella

Bella: Of course.

"We're going to have to do some blood tests," the doctor says upon entering the room. "In emergencies we can get results back sooner from the lab, but you'll still have to stay overnight. We should get the tests back in a matter of hours."

"Thank you," Mom says quietly, and then turns to look at me. "Malcolm, you don't have to stay overnight. I can have your grandmother come pick you up."

I shake my head. "I'm staying."

She reaches forward and gives me a hug. Annie is asleep in the hospital bed beside us with an IV in her wrist. I can't bear to see her this way; so small and fragile in her sleep.

Within a few minutes two nurses come in with needles and vials, and I have to look away. Maybe she's asleep, but I don't want to see them drawing Annie's blood. She's already alarmingly pale as it is.

They leave, and I go back to my phone. I don't have much else to do, and I don't want to think about what could be happening to Annie.

I shoot another text to Bella.

Malcolm: I could really use a distraction right now. Are you busy, or can you talk?

Bella: Of course I can talk. How's Annie doing?

Malcolm: She's asleep right now. They're doing blood tests and we're staying overnight.

Bella: I wish I could visit, but work on our farm is never done. My dad bought my Mom a new horse.

I'm grateful for the distraction. When I talk to Bella, it's like I don't have to worry about the bad things anymore.

Malcolm: That's cool. What's his/her name?

Bella: It's a girl. She's a paint horse named Ginger.

Malcolm: Oh, I see... so Blue has a girlfriend now?

Bella: They've only just met, but they seem to be getting on well. Who knows what the future holds?

Malcolm: Are you still talking about the horses?

Bella: What do you mean?

Malcolm: Never mind XD

Bella and I talk for hours. We only stop so I can eat (hospital food, gag), and then we go right back to texting. I learn ten things about Bella that I didn't know before.

1. She loves studying the stars.

2. She's had four dogs in her life, and her most recent one died a year ago at the age of eighteen.

3. Her older brother is twenty-four and lives with his fiance in NY.

4. She loves roller coasters.

5. Her Dad has been fixing up an old truck for the past year, and she thinks he's going to give it to her for her birthday. If not, she's going to buy a cheap broken one and fix it herself.

6. Her children will be named Rose, Leon and Maisie. In that order.

7. Her favorite book is 'To Kill a Mockingbird.' She says that it teaches important life lessons, and if everyone on Earth read it there might be a chance for world peace.

8. Her fondest childhood memory is wading in the stream and searching for lizards with her brother.

9. She hates tuna fish with a passion.

10. Her personality type is ENFJ-A.

Bella: What's your personality type?

Malcolm: Idk. What is that from?

Bella: It's called the Meyers-Briggs personality test.

Malcolm: I'll check it out. Brb.

Malcolm: I got ISTP-T.

     Eventually I bid her goodnight. Annie hasn't woken up since before the blood tests, and I'm grateful for that. She's peaceful when she sleeps. I don't want her to be afraid.

     I take Annie's hand and lay my head beside hers on the pillow. I don't care if what she has is contagious. Annie is my little sister, and if she has to suffer, I want to be as close to her as I can.

- - -

     I wake up with Annie's hand still in mine, and when I turn to look at her I realize that she's awake. She smiles weakly when she sees me, her lips dry.

     "How are you feeling?" I ask tiredly, sitting up.

     I don't let go of her hand, but with the other I pick up my phone and check the time. It's 3:46 in the morning.

     "I feel a little better," Annie says. Her voice is dry and small, but at least she's being positive.

     Mom's still asleep in the chair across from me by the door, her head against the arm of the chair. She looks uncomfortable.

The door opens, and the doctor peeks her head in. Her eyes go from Annie and I to mom and back again.

"Mom," I say quietly.

Mom blinks, and then takes in the rest of the room. When her eyes fall on the doctor she sits up straighter.

"The results are in," the doctor says. "Mrs. Gibbs, will you come out into the hallway, please?"

Mom looks over at Annie and I, and then stands up shakily. I try to follow, but Annie pulls me back.

"Stay," she whimpers. "Please. I don't want to be alone."

I sit back down, my heart slamming against my chest. This can't be good. 'Come out into the hallway, please?' That's what doctors say when their news could upset the patient.

"I'm really sick, aren't I?" Annie whispers. She doesn't look afraid, just sad.

I squeeze her hand. "You'll be okay."

Annie smiles dryly. "Do you want me to be okay?"

"Of course I do," I say, and put my other hand over hers so I'm holding it in both of mine. "I love you, Annabear."

Annie reaches forward and I hug her, gently so I won't hurt her. It's like I'm afraid that she'll break beneath my hands.

Mom comes back into the room, her eyes distant and unreadable. The doctor motions for me to come into the hall, and Mom takes her turn sitting with Annie. I take a deep breath and follow.

I close the door behind me and wait for the doctor to speak. I lean against the wall, trying to stay calm and finding it to be more difficult than I anticipated.

"Your sister has leukemia," she says.

I mouth the word, but it doesn't make sense. I know I've heard of it, but I can't quite remember what it is.

"Leukemia is cancer of the blood," the doctor continues when I don't speak.

I gape at her. "Cancer?" I shake my head, pushing off the wall and walking a few feet, only to turn around and walk back. "Can you treat her?"

"She'll go through chemotherapy," she says. "The good news is, ninety percent of children with leukemia go through remission and heal. If she's in remission for ten years, she'll be fully out of the danger zone."

"We thought she just had an ear infection," I say weakly.

"Infections are common when a child has leukemia. As is bruising, bleeding, vomiting and some other symptoms. I've already talked to your mother about dieting that will help Annie heal, as well as changes to her lifestyle. Your sister has a good chance of getting through this, Malcolm."

I nod, but don't meet the doctor's eyes.

Chapter Ten

When we get home Mom brings Annie inside, but I decide that I need some fresh air. I grab the old basketball, feeling nostalgic when I think about mine.

But now Bella has it, I remind myself. *And she loves it.*

I dribble the ball for a while and then shoot, but I miss. I throw it again, and it hits the backboard but doesn't go through the net.

Anger burns inside of me, not just because I can't make it through the net but because the world is against me. How can so many awful things happen all at once? It isn't just unfair, it's cruel.

"Are you stress shooting?"

She stands at the edge of her property again, watching me with concern.

I launch the ball again and miss. "Yep. Burning off steam."

"Why are you steaming?"

"You mean steaming hot?" I joke dryly.

Bella frowns. "First of all, isn't it smoking hot?"

"I guess. Second of all?"

"I don't know if I should ask right now, but..." she trails off. "How's Annie? Did you get the lab results?"

I drop the ball and sigh. "Yeah."

"Were they..." she stops mid-sentence. "Do you want to go for a ride?"

I frown. "A car ride?"

"No. I meant a trail ride. You know, horses?"

"Oh. I've never ridden a horse before," I admit.

Bella claps her hands together. "Awesome! I can teach you."

I glance over at the house hesitantly. "Maybe I should tell my Mom where I am so she doesn't worry."

"Okay. I'll go get Blue and Ginger tacked up. Meet me by the pasture's gate."

"Great. See you in a bit."

Bella laughs.

"What?"

"You made an unintentional horse joke," she says with a grin. She shakes her head when my expression remains blank. "Never mind."

- - -

"So you'll ride Blue and I'll ride Ginger," Bella tells me. "Since Ginger isn't used to my family yet, it's better if a more experienced rider rides her."

I nod, wiping my sweaty palms on my jeans. I wouldn't admit it to Bella, but I'm sort of terrified of actually riding a horse. They're nice to look at and talk to, but actually sitting on one's back...

At least it's Blue that I get to ride. If I trust a horse, it's definitely him.

"You're a new rider, so you'll wear a helmet," Bella continues, handing me a black riding helmet. "And just in case you decide that it's too pathetic to be the only one of us with a helmet, I'll wear one too." Bella flips her head back so her hair falls behind her shoulders, then puts the helmet on and buckles it under her chin.

I follow her example (without the hair flipping), before she shows me how to get up. She puts one foot in the stirrup and swings the other leg over, landing cleanly in the saddle and looking down at me. "Your turn."

I don't do it as quickly or as easily as she did, but I manage to get into the saddle.

"Now hold the reins. Make sure you give him some slack. To walk you can either lean forward or softly hit your heels into his sides. To turn right, put the reins on the left side and tug gently. Left is the opposite. Do you understand?"

"Sounds complicated," I say, fumbling with the reins.

"It isn't. Not when you get the hang of it," Bella encourages. "Are you ready?"

"No. I mean, I guess so." I can feel the sweat running down the sides of my face, and I brush it away with the back of my hand.

"You'll do fine," Bella laughs. "Just follow me. We'll take an easy trail through the woods, okay?"

"Okay," I say doubtfully.

Bella leans forward and presses her heels into Ginger's sides, and the horse starts forward. I do the same, and after a moment Blue is following Ginger.

"Can you try to come up beside me?" Bella asks, and she slows down a bit. I lead Blue to Ginger's right, and soon the horses are walking side by side.

"So," I say, out of breath even though Blue's doing all of the work. "What are you doing for your birthday tomorrow?"

"Hey, you remembered," Bella says with a smile.

"Of course I remembered. Do you have plans?"

"My parents are taking me out to dinner, but that's it. They have a lot of work to do during the day. They're horse breeders," she adds. "Their business is based a few miles away. They'll be there until five, so I'll probably be hanging out at home feeling bad for myself."

"Well we can't have that." I think for a moment, and an idea begins to grow in the back of my head. "Meet me at the fence tomorrow at noon."

Bella smiles slowly. "Okay. For what?"

I grin. "You're going to have to trust me."

- - -

We ride for what seems to be hours, but I don't get bored. This saddle is a bit uncomfortable, but I ignore it. I'm with Bella, and that's all that matters.

When I'm with her, I forget that life is unfair.

I forget that I'm insecure.

I forget that I need a therapist because my life is so messed up.

I forget every bad thing that's ever happened.

When I'm with Bella, I can just... live.

"I might as well say it," I murmur.

We're taking the horses through a shallow stream, which might have scared me to death an hour ago. Now I've decided that I trust Blue completely.

"Say what?" Bella asks, looking over.

"About Annie. The lab results?"

Bella's eyes return to the path ahead, and she sighs. "You don't have to tell me if you don't want to."

"But I should. Annie would want me to," I say hesitantly. I know I have to make myself say it, but it feels like saying it out loud makes it more real. "She has cancer. Uh, leukemia. You know, cancer of the blood?"

Bella bites her lip. "God. I'm so sorry, Mal. I mean... can I call you Mal? I don't know why I said it, I just sort of-"

"Yeah, that's fine. I mean, I know it means 'bad' in Spanish, but everyone in my family calls me that." I force a smile. "Maybe that's why they use that nickname."

Bella laughs. "Probably not."

We're both quiet again. The joy feels fake, now that I've mentioned Annie. I have to glance over at Bella a few times to make myself happy again, and even then I feel a sort of emptiness.

"I was thinking," Bella says after a moment. "I mean, I just wanted to ask you something."

"Go ahead."

Bella's face flushes, and she doesn't seem to know what to say. I wait expectantly, but when she speaks she says, "It isn't important."

"Oh, come on Bella. Now I'm going to be curious."

"It's seriously not important," she says, embarrassed.

"Please ask me?"

Bella bites her lip. "I don't know if it's just me. I don't think it's just me, I think you have... as well... um..." She sighs. "What I mean to say is, do you...."

"Yes," I say. "Yes, I do."

"You do what?" She asks. "You might not know what I was-"

"I like you," I interrupt.

She's quiet for a moment, and then she lets out a small laugh.

"That... is what you were asking, isn't it?" I ask awkwardly.

Bella smiles at me. "Yeah. And... I like you too."

Chapter Eleven

I spend the following morning sweeping out the barn. The loft is the most important part to clean, but I don't want the entryway to look messy, either. I sort through the random equipment and trash that's scattered across the floor and stack what I can't throw away neatly in the back room. I bring out a mop and bucket and mop until my hands are sore and the floor is sparkling, and then head up to the loft to clean.

There isn't much up here, and what I do find on the ground is useful. After a few minutes of scavenging I've found two wooden chairs that are in good condition, a spool of white Christmas lights, and a large blue flower pot with only a small chip on the side.

I sweep the hay and other garbage into a disposable bag and throw it away, then work on stringing up the lights and setting up the chairs with a small table I borrowed from the back porch. I set up the flowerpot in the corner of the loft and fill it with wildflowers I picked at the edge of the woods, and then I go inside to find Grandma.

"Will you teach me how to make that bread you made our first night here?" I ask her.

"We're having hotdogs for dinner, so we don't need bread. Do you want to wait until tomorrow and we'll have it with spaghetti and meatballs?"

"I need it today," I say. "For... something else."

Grandma eyes me suspiciously, then smiles. "Alright. Do you want to make anything else?"

"If you don't mind, I have a few thoughts..."

- - -

By twelve o'clock, the table in the loft is set with sandwiches, cookies, brownies and an assortment of fruits.

I hope it's not too much, I think nervously.

I meet Bella at the fence, and she's wearing a blue sundress and sandals. Her hair is down in waves, and a pair of gold-tinted sunglasses sit on top of her head.

"Hey," she says when she sees me.

I give her what I hope is a charming smile. "Happy birthday."

"Happy- I mean, thanks," she says.

I laugh. "I do the same thing."

Bella clasps her hands together, leaning slightly to the side and biting her lip. "So... what are we doing?"

"If you'd follow me, I'll show you," I say, putting out my arm.

She smiles and takes it, and I lead her to the barn. When we get into the loft, Bella lets out a small gasp.

"Wow, Malcolm... did you do all of this?"

"Do you like it?"

Bella smiles. "I can't believe you did all of this for me! No one's ever done something like this for me before."

"Well, you're worth it," I say with a grin. "I hope you're not allergic to walnuts, because I put a lot of sweat and tears into these cookies."

"Er... I'm gluten free, Mal."

My smile falls away. I only stare at her, unable to comprehend what she just said.

"I'm joking!" she says quickly. "I'm only allergic to bees. I'm sorry, I just wanted to see your reaction."

It's all I can do not to wipe tears of relief from my eyes. I pull out a chair for her. "Very funny, Bella. You only gave me a heart attack."

Bella laughs, and after she sits I push her chair in for her.

"Uh, help yourself," I say quickly, gesturing to the food.

Bella smiles and begins to load her plate, not the way that Liv used to (the serving size of a mouse), but the way a growing girl should eat. I sit down across from her and begin to serve myself.

"This bread is delicious!" Bella says after biting into a turkey sandwich.

"My grandmother helped. She's an amazing cook."

"You'll have to give her my thanks," Bella says with a small smile. "You know, your grandmother talks about you all the time."

"She does?" I ask, dismayed. "Great."

Bella laughs. "Not bad things, of course. She brags about you. Your basketball skills, your good looks."

I raise my eyebrows. "Do you agree with her?"

Bella rolls her eyes. "Anyway, I have some news."

"Good news?"

Bella takes a deep breath and sets down her sandwich. "I'm not sure. I think it's good news, but I... I don't know what to do about it." She bites her lip. "I got into NYU."

"Oh."

"Yeah, I know. I should be excited... which, I am! I mean, it's NYU. But..."

"But?"

"It's so far from home," Bella says quietly. "I don't want to leave, now that..." She trails off. "I don't know if I should go or not. It's an amazing opportunity, but... I just don't know."

I pick up my sandwich and make myself take a bite. Now that I'm getting close to Bella... what if she decides to leave? I'll lose one of my only sources of happiness.

"Maybe we should talk about something else," Bella says.

"Okay. Like what?"

Bella smiles. "Like... I was right about that truck?"

"The one your dad was fixing?"

"Yep. It's all mine," Bella says with a proud grin.

"You're lucky. I've had my license for months and I still don't have a car," I say glumly.

"Well, you and I can take turns with mine."

I laugh. "Alright."

"So, I was just wondering," Bella starts, leaning forward and resting her elbows on the table. "Would you call this... a date?"

"Well, we are hanging out, just the two of us. Plus you're crushing on me pretty hard."

Bella glares as me, but her mouth wears a smile.

"So, yes, I'd say it's a date. If you want it to be."

Bella thinks for a moment. "So... is it a casual date?"

"As opposed to...?"

"I don't know, an official one?" Bella says slowly.

"Wait," I say, sitting back a bit. "Bella, are you asking if I want to be your boyfriend?"

"I never said that."

"That's too bad," I say, picking at my sandwich. "I would have said yes." Bella squints at me, so I add, "Bella Monroe, country to my city, apple of my eye, horse whisperer... will you be my girlfriend? To have and to hold, in sickness and in-"

"Malcolm, stop," Bella says, laughing. "Yes, okay? You're a dork, but yes."

- - -

I can't fall asleep. I try counting mind sheep, I try reciting the ABCs forward and backward in my head, but nothing works. I can't stop thinking about Bella.

I've never met anyone like her in my life. She's full of energy and ideas, she's brilliant and she knows what she wants to do with her life, she's funny, she's beautiful... and maybe we're dating right now, but would that change if she went to college?

She'd probably meet a guy who's smarter than I'll ever be, one without so much emotional baggage. She'd make new friends, have new experiences, and I'd just be a memory. I'd be 'the old neighbor.'

Unlike her, I wouldn't have moved on. I'd be in school until I was twenty, I wouldn't go to college, I'd play basketball by myself in my free time... and whenever I looked at the stars, I'd think of Bella. I'd think of her when I saw fireworks, calm water, cookies and horses. I'd think of her when I went to the library, when I walked through meadows and when I saw cowboy boots. I'd see her in all of the beautiful things, the things that lessen the load of pain life presses on the world.

"Mom!"

It's Annie.

"Mom!" She cries again, and I hear a thud.

At first I think I'm dreaming, but the sound of footsteps crashing into Annie's room is far too real. I sit up in bed and yank off my sheets, before racing from the room to see what's going on.

Chapter Twelve

The world is an awful thing. People say that the good balances the bad, but it doesn't. The good is stolen from the bad, until only the darkness remains.

"Annie, everything's okay," I'm saying over and over. I clutch her hand so she has something to hold on to as the gurney is wheeled to the emergency room. Mom holds her other hand, and whispers soothing words like my own. Annie moans and clutches her abdomen, and I wish that I could do something to take away her pain.

"We're going to have to take it from here," a tall doctor says to Mom and I. "No one besides the patient and the doctors are allowed beyond this point," he adds apologetically.

"But she'll be so frightened!" Mom pleads.

"She'll be given soothing medicines to keep her calm during surgery," the doctor says patiently.

"Surgery?" I repeat. "What's going on?"

"We will send someone in to explain the situation to both of you," the doctor says. "Excuse me, but we really do have to work quickly." He turns and the four of them wheel Annie through a wide doorway and the door swings shut behind them.

I've never felt so far away from her... so useless. I can't help her. I can't do anything but wait. I don't say a word, I only follow Mom into the waiting room and sit. I'm silent when Mom offers me a tray of food, only shaking my head.

As the doctor promised, a nurse enters the waiting room and comes to talk to Mom and I. When I see her expression, I clench the sides of my chair until my knuckles go white.

"Sometimes leukemia can cause the spleen to expand, and it can get in the way of other organs. That's why Annie was experiencing abdominal pain," she explains.

"So they're going to remove it?" Mom asks quietly.

The nurse nods. "It normally takes two to four hours, and the recovery process should be a few weeks if all goes well."

"If all goes well?" I repeat. "And how likely is it that it will?"

The nurse stares at me for a moment, before replying, "The success rate is about sixty percent."

- - -

Bella and her parents arrive half an hour later.

"We came as soon as we heard," Bella's mother says, giving Mom a hug. "Is there anything we can do?"

They continue talking, and Bella comes to sit beside me. She takes my hand in hers and squeezes it. "I'm here for you, okay? You aren't alone."

"Yeah, but Annie is," I mumble.

Bella lays her head on my shoulder and puts her arms around me, and a small wave of peace washes over me, only to be taken over by pain a moment later. "Why does all of the bad stuff happen to the people around me, but never me?"

"I don't know," Bella murmurs. "But I'm glad nothing bad is happening to you. I know, it's selfish. But I really am."

I press my lips against her cheek gently. "At least you're okay. I don't know what I'd do without you," I whisper.

"You'd do whatever you did before you met me."

I close my eyes, resting my forehead against her hair. "I can't even remember my life before I met you."

- - -

When I wake up it's early morning, and Bella's still sitting beside me holding my hand. Her sleeping parents are on the other side of the room, and Mom and Grandma are across from us.

I can imagine all of the looks Bella and I got last night, but I don't care. If I have to deal with all of this crap, I might as well enjoy the good moments without being self-conscious about them.

A doctor walks into the room and says, "Mrs. Gibbs?"

Mom stands up. "Can I see her?"

"Yes, as can her brother," he says, and I stand as well.

"How about her grandmother?" Grandma asks.

"I'm sorry, but only immediate family right now. You can visit her soon."

Grandma sighs and sits back down.

"Malcolm?" Bella says sleepily when I start to follow Mom out of the room. "My parents and I will probably leave when they wake up… But text me if you need anything."

"I will," I say quietly. "Thank you, Bella."

"You're welcome. Tell Annie I'm rooting for her."

- - -

Annie's worse than I've seen her yet. She's ghost-white, with purple skin under her sleepy eyes and what seem to be a million tubes protruding from her arms and nose.

"Malcolm," she whispers when we walk in.

Not Mom, not Jackson... Malcolm.

It's this thing that brings me to my knees beside her, and the tears are falling down my face like rain. I bury my face in the sheet, and feel Annie's hand close around mine.

"Don't cry," Annie whimpers, and tears of her own start to run down her cheeks.

"Then don't you cry, either." I wipe them from her cheek, gently. She feels so delicate, like the softest touch will break her into hundreds of pieces.

Her eyes are glued to my face when she murmurs, "I like you better when you aren't a jerk."

I put my hand over hers carefully. "I like me better when I'm not a jerk, too," I admit.

"So why don't you be nice?"

I wish it was that simple. I wish I was the kind of person who can look at the world wearing a smile and find the good in bad things. But I'm not. I'm me, Malcolm Gibbs, and I'm probably as much of a jerk as my Dad is.

I don't say this to Annie, because I have to help her to see the good even when I can't. "I will from now on."

Annie opens her mouth slowly, and her lips are so dry and white that I think they'll crack. "Do you promise?" She croaks.

"I promise."

Annie forces a smile. "Good. And... I won't be a brat anymore, okay? I promise too."

"Oh Annie," I whisper, and the tears are back. "You aren't a brat. I was just being a jerk when I said that."

"I'm a brat sometimes," Annie sighs. "I think everyone is."

"That's because no one's perfect," I say quickly, rubbing her pale cheek with my thumb. "But you, Annie? You're as close as you can be."

Annie smiles. "So are you, Malcolm."

- - -

She just seems to be getting worse. Mom isn't telling me anything, but I can hear it in her tone when she talks to doctors outside of the waiting room and I can see it in her expression.

On our fourth day at the hospital, Mom finally says something, but it doesn't have to do with Annie.

"I want you to go home with your Grandmother," she tells me. "You haven't gotten enough sleep lately, and it isn't good for you to sit around the hospital for days waiting."

"But if something happens-"

"Then you can drive straight here. Grandma will let you use her car, I'm sure," she says. "Right, Mom?"

"Of course," Grandma replies, standing from her chair. "What do you say, Malcolm?"

"I think I should stay here."

"Malcolm, I want you to go home," Mom says more forcefully. "I tried to give you the choice, but you aren't thinking. This isn't good for you... not mentally or physically. You already haven't seen Dr. Waterman in over a week-"

"Oh, so I'm so mentally unstable that I can't handle not seeing a therapist for that long?" I challenge, and the lack of sleep makes me angrier. "If my little sister dies, maybe I want to be here. I couldn't stay with Jackson, but now I have the choice to be with Annie... and you're trying to take it away from me!"

"Annie is not going to die," Mom says stiffly.

"Oh yeah? Since when are you God, Mom? He took Jackson, he took Grandpa, he separated you and Dad... and you know what? He might as well take me too!" I yell.

"Malcolm, you get out of this hospital right now," Mom whispers, tears brimming in her eyes.

"Fine," I mutter, and I do as she says.

Chapter Thirteen

Neither of us say anything on the way home. Grandma sits in the driver's seat with her jaw clenched, like she's gritting her teeth to keep from giving me a talking to. Maybe I should feel ashamed of myself, but I don't.

I don't care about anything anymore.

What about Bella? My calmer side urges.

Bella's going to go to NYU. Of course, she'll have to break up with me first. *Yet another thing that I can't control.*

My heart starts beating harder in my frustration.

It's no longer my mind in control, but my actions. I feel reckless. The worst that can happen is already happening, so why would I care about the consequences? What have I got to lose?

"Are you going to be okay?" Grandma asks once we've parked. It's the first thing she's said since she agreed to let me use her car.

Her car!

"I will be," I say quickly. "I'm going to play some basketball. It helps me relieve stress."

Grandma nods. "I'll be in my garden if you need me." She puts out her arms and gives me a hug. "I love you, Malcolm."

"I love you too, Grandma." I feel a pang of guilt about what I'm going to do, but then I push it away.

I get my basketball and start shooting, hoping that Grandma leaves her keys on the counter like she usually does instead of bringing them to the garden with her. I'm about to go inside and check, when I hear Bella's voice.

"Malcolm," she says, and runs to me. I'm too numb to move when she puts her arms around me, and I can barely feel the warmth she lets off.

"I think you should go," I mutter, remembering that she's going to dump me and leave to go to NYU in the fall.

You don't know that for sure, my practical side hisses.

I know that my life sucks, so yeah, I know that for sure, I think back.

Bella steps back. "Sorry, you probably need space," she says, but I can hear the hurt in her voice. "I understand."

"No, you don't understand," I reply bitterly. "You'll never understand. Your life is perfect. You have good grades, you're nice, you know who you are. You have *no idea* what it's like."

Bella only stares at me, her eyes wide and her mouth parted as if she's about to speak but can't.

"It doesn't matter," I continue. "I'll make it easy for both of us. We should stop seeing each other."

Hurt flashes across Bella's face, and she whispers, "This isn't you talking, Malcolm. It's your pain. Please, just think about this."

"I'm done thinking," I growl. "Thinking doesn't keep bad things from happening. It doesn't keep your world from breaking apart."

"So you're just going to break it?" Bella asks, tears rising in her eyes. "Just so you can be in control?"

"Goodbye, Bella," I say, dropping the ball.

Bella looks at me for a few seconds, tears running down her cheeks. Finally she turns and walks away, her back straight and her chin up.

At least it's not me who has to hurt anymore, I think selfishly. *Let someone else have a turn.*

- - -

The keys are exactly where I thought they'd be. I scoop them up in my palm and hurry from the room, just in case Grandma comes back.

Not that she'd be able to stop me. Honestly, I don't think anyone could stop me at this point.

I just want to go for a ride. I want to see where the road takes me. Maybe I'm too reckless for driving, but that's what makes me want to do it. I'm stealing my Grandmother's car and hitting the road.

I start the car and peel out of the driveway much faster than I should, and I'm gliding down the road a moment later.

I wonder if Grandma heard the engine. I wonder if she's calling Mom. I wonder if Mom would tell Annie. I wonder if Annie's dead.

I haven't seen rain since we moved to Kentucky, but it's as if it suddenly breaks loose from the sky. It pelts my windshield, so thick that I can barely see. The windshield wipers are swishing back and forth frantically, but they aren't much help. I begin to wonder if God is unleashing his fury upon me for what I've done.

But think of all of the things that you did to me! I want to scream to the sky. *You've taken away everyone I love. Why am I alive? Why don't you take me like you took Jackson?*

Tears are blurring my vision, not that I could see through the windshield anyway. For just an instant, panic sets in. I feel the car beneath me swerve, and I realize that the road is turning but I can't see which way.

Fight back, Jackson whispers.

Goosebumps run up my arms, and I shiver. I feel like the rain is pouring on me, even though I'm inside of the car.

It swerves again, and this time I feel the impact. The car smashes into a tree, but it's small enough to break through it. The car is off-road, and the hill is too steep to stop. I try the brakes, but too quickly. The next thing I know the car is tilting forward and flipping over, and everything disappears.

Chapter Fourteen

The next few weeks are a blur, but I'm alive. I'm in the hospital, and I don't spend one moment by myself. Usually it's Mom who sits beside me, and sometimes even Grandma. They tell me things that are going on, but I can't make myself speak back. Mom explains that I have a neck injury and I won't be able to talk comfortably for a while, but I'll be better in a few weeks. She tells me to just hang in there.

When I ask about Annie, she says that she's still recovering but she looks much better. It isn't long before Annie is well enough to come see me herself.

"Now it's my turn to help you get better," She tells me, and she becomes my new favorite doctor. She spends most of our visits telling me stories. Stories about dinosaurs, astronauts, aliens, ballerinas, and most of all, horses.

My heart is sore when I think about Bella and the way I hurt her. I want to apologize, but she hasn't visited. Even if she did, I don't know if I would be able to speak to her.

"I saw Bella riding Blue this morning," Annie says one day. "She looked lonely. I think she misses you." Then she puts her lips close to my ear and whispers, "I just wanted to tell you, I think you and Bella should get married. Then I can ride her horses all the time and she'll be like my sister."

The day finally comes when the doctors let me go home. I still have to recover for another week or two, but my throat feels a lot better.

Annie hangs out in my room for a while before she gets bored and takes a 'babysitting break.' I sit in my bed and think about my life, about all of the things I was wrong about and all of the things I wish I could do differently.

It's so dark in here.

I stand up and carefully make my way to the balcony, drawing open the curtains and opening the door so I can inhale the fresh air of late summer.

The neighing of a horse brings me out onto the balcony. I look down at the three of them, Ginger, Blue and Bella. The horses seem to be having a conversation while they eat, which makes me smile. Bella's sitting in the grass a few yards away, looking very lonely and distant as she picks at the weeds around her.

My voice still isn't well enough to call to her, so I bring my fingers to my mouth and let out a sharp whistle.

Bella and the horses look up, but the horses go back to grazing. Bella, on the other hand, stands up and looks at me.

I put up a hand as if to tell her to 'wait right there,' and leave the balcony. I hurry downstairs and out the front door despite Mom's telling me to slow down, and meet Bella at the fence.

"I'm so sorry," I say, my voice cracking. "I'm the biggest jerk ever and I don't deserve you, but what I did... I regret it more than anything I've ever done. I understand if you don't forgive me, but..." I take a deep breath, and grab hold of her hands over the fence. "Bella... I love you. I've never loved someone before, not really. You're different than anyone I've ever met."

Bella studies my eyes for a few moments, her expression unreadable. Then she leans forward and kisses me, her hands still in mine. My surprise subsides and I kiss her back, and I decide that I'll trade all of the other good things in life for this girl in a heartbeat.

Epilogue

Bella and I lay in the back of her truck, looking up at the starry night sky.

It will be fall in a few weeks, so we're savoring the last of summer together while it lasts. Bella will be attending Kentucky State University, which I was relieved to learn is only fifteen minutes away. I, of course, will be going to high school.

Annie is in remission, and she looks as healthy as she did before she got sick. I've recovered from my injuries, and I've gone back to seeing Dr. Waterman.

Generally, I'm a much happier person. I'm not saying this because I'm with Bella (even though she makes me pretty freaking happy), and I'm not saying it because Annie's getting better. I'm saying it because I've learned so much about life over the past few months.

I pick up my journal and pen and begin to write an entry, which is long overdue. Bella's the kind of girlfriend who watches over your shoulder while you write, but I don't mind.

Dear Jackson,

I've realized that life isn't so bad, after all. It seems like it sometimes, like all of the bad things have become so heavy that you can't bear the weight, but the people who love you will help you carry it if you ask them to. Those are the people who will always watch out for you, even when you think you don't want them to. They're the people who you share your best (and worst) moments with. They're the ones who lift you up when you're sad and stand with you no matter what. I have many of these people in my life. Grandma, Mom, Annie, and Bella. Maybe you can't control life, but you can control your actions when life hits you. It isn't always the score that counts in basketball, it's how you play the game.

Thank you for helping me to realize that life is what you make it out to be. You tried to teach me that my whole life, and I only understand it now.

Life is about playing tag with your little sister. It's about cooking food with your grandmother. It's about being strong for your mother so she can put faith in you. It's about not giving up when bad things happen. It's about sitting in the back of a pickup truck and watching the stars light up the face of the girl you love.

- Malcolm

About the Author

Carynn M. Bohley is a teenage author from Upstate NY. She lives on a farm with her parents, four younger siblings, and many (many) animals.

She is currently a college student, and has many hobbies ranging from writing to singing to movie making.

Her biggest goal is to write a book that makes you laugh, cry, and leaves you wanting more.

Made in the USA
Monee, IL
15 August 2022

11658524R00069